DATE DUE

I Am Good at Being Me

LITTLE SIMON INSPIRATIONS

An imprint of Simon & Schuster Children's Publishing Division

1230 Avenue of the Americas, New York, New York 10020

Text copyright © 2005 by Karen Hill

Illustrations copyright © 2005 by Renee Graef

All rights reserved, including the right of reproduction

in whole or in part in any form.

LITTLE SIMON INSPIRATIONS and associated colophon

are trademarks of Simon & Schuster, Inc.

Manufactured in the United States of America

First Edition

2 4 6 8 10 9 7 5 3 1

ISBN 1-4169-0512-X

Scripture taken from the *Holy Bible, New International Version*

copyright © 1973, 1978, 1984 by International Bible Society.

Used by permission of Zondervan Bible Publishers.

I Am Good at Being Me

By Karen Hill

Illustrated by Renee Graef

LITTLE SIMON INSPIRATIONS

New York   London   Toronto   Sydney

For Lindsey—you breathe life into this verse—"children are the gift of the Lord." (PSALM 127: 3) —K. H.

For Victoria —R. G.

"Let everything
that has breath
praise the Lord."
(Psalm 150: 6)

A great pine tree stood tall and proud, deep in the forest. The tree could see for miles around . . . mountains, rivers, and all the forest animals that wandered by.

"I'm special," said the tree. "God made me big and tall so I can give shade. I'm good at being a pine tree."

A prickly pinecone plunked to the ground.

"I'm special too," said the pinecone. "God made me so there will be a new tree someday. I am good at being a pinecone."

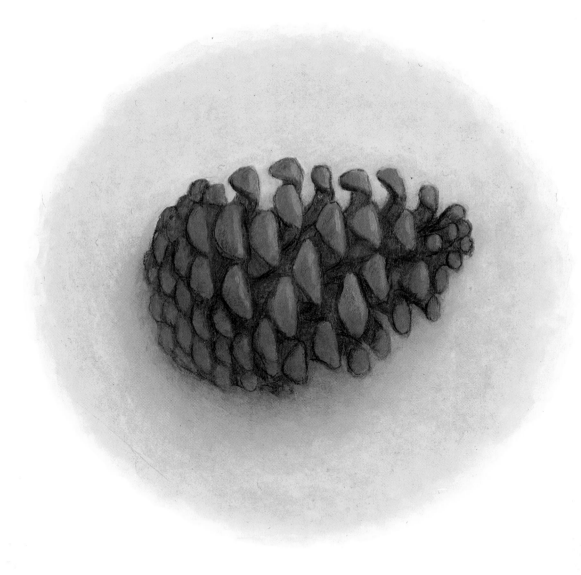

A pine needle broke off the great tree and floated down, down to the ground below.

"Well, I may be just a needle, but I'm special too. God made me to feed the soil. I am good at being a pine needle."

The third branch from the top of the tree
stood very still in the breeze. "Don't forget me.
I'm really special. God made me to hold the
birds' nests. I am a good nest-holder."

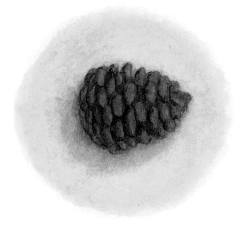
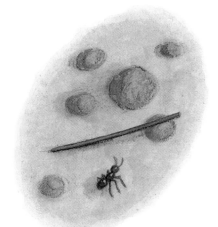

And so it went.

The tree, the pinecone, the pine needle, and the branch each knew God's special plan for them. And knowing their purpose made them happy.

It was a good day in the forest.

Until . . . the great tree heard something sniffling in its branches.

It was a small bird in the high nest.

"What's wrong, little fella?" asked the tree.

"I . . . uh . . .," started the bird, "well, it seems like everyone is special but me. I don't know why God made me."

The tall pine stretched its branches and thought for a moment.

"Little Bird, I'm sure that God has a plan for everything, and he has a special purpose for you, too."

"But I'm not pretty like the bluebird," sighed the bird. "My wings aren't fast like the hummingbird. I can't fly high like the eagle. I don't do anything special."

"God will help you understand why he made you," said the wise old tree. "But now it's getting late. Little Bird, go to sleep."

And so the forest settled down for the night.

When morning came, there was something
new in the forest. The great pine tree heard it
first. A sweet, sweet melody.

"What's that sound?" wondered the tree.

Squirrels stopped stashing acorns to listen.

Caterpillars quit munching leaves to listen.

Deer stopped prancing to listen.

The whole forest listened to the wonderful song.

Who could be making that beautiful music?

It was the little bird.

"Little Bird!" said the tree. "I know why you're special. God made you to sing. And you are very good at singing!"

Little Bird sang his new song again.

"God made me, it's plain to see . . . He gave me wings and a song to sing. . . ."

From that day on, Little Bird filled the forest with the special song God had given him. And Little Bird was happy.

24